MARVEL STUDIOS

THOR

THE MOVIE STORYBOOK

Adapted by Elizabeth Rudnick
Based on the screenplay by Ashley Edward Miller & Zack Stentz and Don Payne
Story by J. Michael Straczynski and Mark Protosevich

Published by Marvel Press, an imprint of Disney Publishing Worldwide. No part of this book may be reproduced or transmitted in any form or by any means, electronic or mechanical, including photocopying, recording, or by any information storage and retrieval system, without written permission from the publisher. For information address
Marvel Press, 114 Fifth Avenue, New York, New York 10011-5690.

Printed in the United States of America

First Edition

1 3 5 7 9 10 8 6 4 2

V381-8386-5-11046

ISBN 978-1-4231-4312-3

The sun shone brightly over the majestic Realm of Asgard. Inside the royal palace, servants bustled between rooms, setting up banquet tables, placing wine goblets, and greeting the honored guests. In their chambers, the royal family prepared for a very special ceremony.

Today, Odin Allfather, king of Asgard, would pass the throne to his son, Thor.

In a smaller room, away from the hustle and bustle, the Warriors Three gathered. Volstagg the Voluminous, whose vast passions matched his huge size, combed his beard. Fandral the Fair, a charismatic swashbuckler, appreciated his own reflection. And as usual, Hogun the Grim stood apart, his expression sullen. These three were not only the strongest and mightiest of Asgard's soldiers—they were also Thor's best friends. They had gone on countless adventures with him—and saved Thor on more than one occasion.

Suddenly a door opened and the Lady Sif entered. Walking over to a small table, she put down her double-bladed sword and removed several daggers hidden in her armor. "I'll miss you," Sif said when she was done.

Turning, she joined the others. It was time to go to the ceremony.

The throne room was full of Asgard's most honored citizens. Ceremonial banners adorned the walls, and an excited murmur filled the room as everyone waited for the ceremony to begin. Lady Sif and the Warriors Three took their places and waited.

"I hope this goes quickly," Volstagg whispered. "I'm famished."

Fandral raised an eyebrow. "Noooo," he said, feigning disbelief. His friend could be in the middle of a battle, and he'd still be thinking about food.

"Are you attached to that pretty face of yours?" Volstagg asked. "Because one more word and you won't be."

He looked serious for only a moment before laughing.

Fandral joined in, and then, turning, he looked at Hogun. "Go on, smile," he said. "You can do it."

Hogun's face didn't even twitch.

Hogun was still looking grim when Queen Frigga and her younger son, Loki, entered the room and took their places. A moment later, a horn sounded and guards parted to reveal Odin Allfather sitting atop his golden throne. After everyone was in place, the mighty Thor appeared.

Striding down the long aisle, Thor's blond hair shone beneath his winged helmet, and his red cape flowed behind him. When he was in front of his father, he kneeled, but not before giving his friends a wink.

"A new day has come for a new king to wield his own weapon," Odin began, his voice booming over the room. "Today, I entrust you with the sacred throne of Asgard. Responsibility, duty, honor. They are essential to every soldier . . . and every king."

Suddenly, a chill had come over the room.

Thor was about to be made king when the
chill turned truly frosty. Suddenly, the banners
that hung from the ceiling began to ice over.
The Allfather clutched his spear.

"Frost Giants," Odin said, his voice full
of worry.

Before Volstagg could stop him, Thor
raced out of the room. Volstagg knew that food
was going to have to wait. He and the others
quickly followed after Thor.

They found Thor in the Vault. The large,
underground cavern held all of Asgard's
greatest treasures—as well as its spoils of war. It
was usually guarded by Asgard's elite military
force, the Eiherjar.

Now, two such guards lay on the floor in
front of where the Casket of Ancient Winters
was usually kept. Their bodies were frozen
solid. Looking over, Volstagg saw a black metal
creature standing guard in the shadows. A fiery
glow seemed to come from within it. It held the
casket in its arms.

"The Destroyer," Sif said in awe.

"I thought it was but legend," Volstagg said as the fearsome Destroyer returned the casket to its pedestal and moved back to its post.

"The Frost Giants must pay for what they've done!" Thor interrupted.

Odin looked at his son with troubled eyes. Thor's action could cause a war.

The king nodded to Volstagg and the others, indicating they should leave the Vault. Odin would speak with his son alone.

A short while later, Volstagg made his way to the banquet hall, the others following. It was where the celebration dinner was to have been. Thor and Loki were already there, and it was clear that Thor was angry. As Volstagg watched, Thor flipped over a banquet table, sending food and drink flying.

"Redecorating, are we?" Sif said, her tone teasing but gentle.

Volstagg had other concerns. "All this food," he said sadly. "So innocent. Cast to the ground. It breaks the heart."

Thor ignored them both. His father had forbidden him to take revenge. But Odin was a weak old man.

Thor's gaze then fell on Mjolnir, his hammer. Suddenly a gleam came into his eyes. "We're going to Jotunheim."

"It's madness!" Loki said, trying to reason with his brother.

"Of all the laws of Asgard," Sif said, trying to calm her friend, "this is the one you must not break."

"This isn't like a journey to Earth, where you summon a little lightning and thunder, and the mortals worship you as a god," Fandral pointed out.

"My friends," Thor said, "have you forgotten all that we've done together?" He turned to Hogun. "Who led you into the most glorious of battles?" Then he locked his gaze on Volstagg. "And to delicacies so succulent you thought you'd died and gone to Valhalla?"

Volstagg and Hogun looked sheepish. "You did," they both replied.

Thor nodded as he looked at Fandral and Sif. "My friends, trust me now," he said with determination. "We must do this."

The warriors exchanged looks. Thor was a hard man to say no to. It appeared they were going to Jotunheim.

"I fear we'll live to regret this," Sif said as Thor left the room.

"If we're lucky," Volstagg responded.

The next morning, Thor, Loki, the Warriors Three, and Sif walked across the palace grounds to where their horses and gear waited. Hogun noticed Loki briefly slip away. Hogun did not say anything, but he wondered what the younger prince was doing.

When they had all mounted, Thor looked at his companions. "We must first find a way to get past Heimdall," he said. Heimdall guarded the Rainbow Bridge and controlled the Bifrost— which was the portal that would take them to the Realm of Jotunheim.

"That will be no easy task," Volstagg said. "It's said the gatekeeper can see a single dewdrop from a thousand worlds away."

Fandral raised an eyebrow. Volstagg's stories were as big as his appetite. "And he can hear a cricket in Niffelheim," he said, teasing his friend.

With Volstagg frightened and the others laughing, the group raced off across the Rainbow Bridge to Heimdall's Observatory, leaving the safety of Asgard behind.

They quickly arrived at the Observatory. The bronze, domed building appeared to float in the mists at the end of the Realm, its sides carved with intricate drawings.

Heimdall was waiting for them, blocking their entrance. His stern, intimidating face was partially concealed by his mighty armor. When he turned his gaze on them, Volstagg gulped.

"You think you can deceive me? I, who can hear a cricket in Niffelheim." As he spoke, Heimdall stared knowingly at Fandral. "Never before has an enemy slipped by my watch. I wish to know how that happened."

"Then tell no one where we've gone until we've returned," Thor said. He strode up the stairs and into the Observatory. The others followed, a little less confidently.

The domed room was empty but for a large control panel. Heimdall walked over and in one smooth motion, inserted his sword into the device. The observation room began to turn, and one side opened, revealing the cosmos. Heimdall worked the controls and a blast of rainbow light—the Bifrost—blasted into the black of space.

"All is ready," he said. "You may pass."

"Couldn't you just leave the bridge open for us?" Volstagg asked hopefully.

"To keep this bridge open would unleash the full power of the Bifrost and destroy Jotunheim—with you upon it," Heimdall answered.

Volstagg gulped again. "Ah. Never mind then," he said as they stepped into the portal and disappeared.

In Jotunheim, a large hole opened in the sky. Suddenly, six figures fell out of it and landed on the frozen ground below. Once a beautiful world, Jotunheim was now an icy wasteland, slowly crumbling and breaking apart. In the distance, Thor and his friends could see the ruins of what must have been the Jotun capital city.

"We shouldn't be here," Hogun said, voicing the others' thoughts.

"Too late now," Thor said. "It's time to act."

Then, without another word, he set out in the direction of the capital. He had to find the king of the Jotuns.

The wind howled and ice pelted their faces as they made their way across the Realm. Despite his warm gear, Volstagg shivered, but Thor seemed fine.

"It feels good, doesn't it?" he said cheerfully. "To be together again, adventuring on another world."

"Is that what we're doing?" Fandral asked, his teeth chattering.

"What would you call it?" Thor said.

"Freezing," Fandral replied.

"Starving," Volstagg added

At long last, they reached the ancient city. Structures made of ice were melting and crumbling, the result of a war that had long ago destroyed this Realm. The Asgardians walked further into the ruins, on high alert. But no one was there.

"Where are they?" Sif wondered.

"Hiding," Thor answered, "as cowards always do."

The Frost Giants appeared suddenly, as if from the ice itself. They immediately surrounded the intruders.

"What is your business here?" one of them growled.

Thor raised his head high. "I speak only to your king," he said boldly.

Out of the corner of his eye, Volstagg noticed Loki cringe at his brother's tone.

"Then speak," another voice answered.

Turning to the direction of the voice, the group saw an intimidating blue-skinned figure. "I am Laufey, king of this Realm."

"I demand answers," Thor said. "How did your people get into Asgard?"

"The house of Odin is full of traitors," the king said.

The Warriors Three and Sif exchanged confused glances.

"Do not dishonor my father's name with your lies!" Thor shouted, his temper flaring.

Loki sensed that his brother's self-control was slipping. "Stop and think," Loki said, nodding to the Frost Giants around them. "We are outnumbered."

Thor's jaw clenched, and the others waited with baited breath. Finally, he nodded. They would leave.

But as they turned to go, one of the giants muttered, "Run back home, little princess."

Thor stopped in his tracks.

Reluctantly, the Asgardians drew their weapons and formed a circle around Thor. The Frost Giants prepared for battle as well. Ice formed on their bodies, creating frozen armor.

As Fandral watched, ice covered the length of one of the Frost Giants' arms, forming a sword. "I'm hoping that's just decorative," he said nervously.

As the battle began, the warriors stayed in their circle, slashing and stabbing at the Frost Giants. They had only one goal—to keep Thor safe. But Thor wanted to fight. Stepping outside the circle, he took on several giants at once.

The others closed ranks as the battle continued. The Frost Giant in front of Hogun hurled his ice-sword, but just before it hit Hogun, the warrior raised his mace and slammed it into the ice above. Then he pulled himself up and over the giant. In one smooth move, he leaped down behind him and finished off the giant.

There was no rest for the warriors. Sif fought off Frost Giant after Frost Giant with her double-bladed sword, and Loki relied on his tricks to confuse another Frost Giant and push him into a deep crevasse. Meanwhile, Thor was fighting the Brute, the Jotun's biggest warrior. But the Brute proved no match for the mighty Thor, who made quick work of him and rejoined the others in battle.

A bit further away, Volstagg and Fandral were fighting several giants at once. "You may want to put some ice on that!" Volstagg cried when he got in a particularly good hit. But just then another giant reached out and grabbed him, his fingers closing in on Volstagg's bare arm. Immediately, the skin began to darken as it froze.

"Don't let them grab you!" Volstagg warned the others before pulling away from the giant and retreating.

Meanwhile, Fandral was running into trouble, too. A Frost Giant snapped the Asgardian's sword in half.

"Could we just stop for a moment while I get another sword?" Fandral asked.

In response, the Frost Giant reached into a pool of non-frozen water. With a quick flick of his wrist, he sent a large spray flying into the air. It instantly froze, creating sharp ice spears. Fandral tried to get out of the way when one of the spikes stabbed him.

Volstagg saw his friend get wounded and rushed over to help.

"How's the face?" Fandral asked faintly.

"Flawless," Volstagg said, trying to sound calm. Carefully, he picked up his fellow warrior and placed him over his shoulder. They had to get back to the Bifrost!

Turning, the Asgardians began to run. But Thor continued to fight.

He held Mjolnir, his mighty hammer, up high in the air, then slammed it down on the frozen ground. BOOM! The planet shook from the force of the blow. Instantly the ice began to crack even more.

"What's Thor done?" Volstagg asked as they ran for safety. But he knew the answer. Thor had doomed them all.

The others had just reached the Bifrost site when they looked behind them to see Thor flying over the Realm. Several Frost Giants followed him.

Thor, Loki, Sif, and the Warriors Three had nowhere else to run. They had reached the very edge of the icy world and were quickly surrounded. Hundreds and hundreds of Frost Giants stood at the ready, with Laufey at the front, an evil smile on his face. This looked like the end of the Asgardians.

Suddenly, the air above them crackled and sparked, and a large hole opened in the sky. The sound of thundering hooves filled the air. Then Odin appeared, riding his eight-legged horse, Sleipnir.

He landed and rode over to Laufey, ignoring his sons and the warriors. "You and I can stop this before there's further bloodshed," Odin said to the other king. But Laufey refused. This would mean war.

Odin had to act fast. The Allfather slammed Gungnir, his mighty spear, on the ice, sending the Frost Giants flying backward!

Then, without another word, he took the Asgardians back to Asgard and shut the Bifrost behind him.

Back in the observatory, Odin turned to Thor, furious. His son had deliberately disobeyed him and almost caused a war. This was unacceptable.

"You're a vain, greedy, cruel boy!" Odin said, his heart breaking at each word.

"And you are an old man and a fool!" Thor responded harshly.

Odin's shoulders sagged and his eyes grew sad. "I was a fool to think you were ready." Odin knew what must be done. "You are unworthy of this realm," he began. "Unworthy of your title."

Then Odin looked Thor directly in the eyes as he cried, "In the name of my father, and of his father before, I cast you out!"

Behind them, the Bifrost opened and a shaft of rainbow light blasted into space. A moment later, the bridge closed.

Thor had been banished.

Later that day, Sif and the Warriors Three gathered in the Palace's healing room. They sat before a roaring fire and used healing stones to cure their injuries.

"We should never have let him go," Volstagg said, breaking the silence.

"At least he's only banished, not dead," Fandral said, trying to find some good in the situation. If Odin hadn't saved them, they might not have survived the battle. They had gotten lucky—but that luck was quickly running out.

After a moment, Hogun finally spoke. "Laufey said there were traitors in the house of Odin."

Volstagg and Fandral turned to their fellow warrior, shocked. "Why is it every time you choose to speak, it has to be something dark and ominous?" Fandral asked.

The grim warrior did not reply at first. He had not spoken lightly. He knew that what he said verged on treason.

"The ceremony was interrupted just before Thor was named king," Volstagg said.

"We should go to Allfather," Sif said. "It's our duty. If any of our suspicions are right and there is a traitor, then all of Asgard is in danger."

Soon, the group found themselves standing in front of the throne room. Two guards stood at the entrance. Seeing Sif and the Warriors Three, they nodded and opened the doors.

Bursting in, they kept their heads bowed as they walked to the front of the room. "Allfather," Sif said, "we must speak to you—urgently."

Slowly, she and the warriors raised their heads. Their eyes grew wide and they nearly gasped. Loki stood before Odin's throne holding the Allfather's spear in his hand.

"What is this?" Volstagg said in disbelief.

"My friends, you haven't heard?" Loki said, acting surprised though he knew they had no way of knowing what he was about to say. "I am now ruler of Asgard. Father's fallen into the Odinsleep. My mother fears he may never awaken again."

The Warriors Three and Lady Sif were unsure of how to proceed. Anyone could be the traitor.

"We would speak with your mother," Sif finally said.

"She has refused to leave my father's bedside," Loki replied. "You can bring your 'urgent' matter to me—your king."

This was not going according to plan. Sif thought quickly. "We would ask you to end Thor's banishment," she said. That sounded like something they would have come to speak to Odin about.

Loki shook his head. "My first command cannot be to undo the Allfather's last." He smiled down at them, a knowing gleam in his eye. "All of us must stand together, for the good of Asgard."

Then, with a nod of his head, he dismissed them.

A short while later, the group was back in the palace healing room. Volstagg sat in front of a platter of food, ravenously eating. Sif stood nearby, looking ill at ease. Fandral watched Volstagg stuff himself.

"Our dearest friend banished, Loki on the throne, Asgard on the brink of war, yet you manage to consume four wild boar, six pheasant, a side of beef, and two casks of ale," Fandral said, disbelieving. "Don't you care?"

Volstagg glared at the other warrior. "Do not mistake my appetite for apathy!" he said, his jaw clenched.

"We must go," Hogun said, deciding their next course of action. It was treason to do what they were about to do. But the only way to save Asgard was to find Thor. Turning, Hogun was about to leave when two guards entered the room. The others froze.

"Heimdall demands your presence," one of the guards announced.

Volstagg finished his ale. "We're doomed," he said, wiping his mouth.

When the four reached the Observatory, they found Heimdall standing at the Bifrost's controls. He stared at them accusingly.

"You would defy the command of Loki, our king, break every oath you have taken as warriors, and commit treason to bring Thor back?" he asked.

"Yes, but—" Sif began nervously.

"Good," Heimdall said, confusing them.

"I am bound by honor to our king," he went on. "I cannot open the Bifrost to you." Turning, he left the Observatory.

For a moment, there was nothing but silence. Until . . . "Look!" Sif cried. Heimdall had left his sword in the control panel! It seemed the guardian wanted to help them after all.

They were going to find Thor. But to which Realm had he been banished? Cautiously, they stepped into the Bifrost, unsure of where they would end up.

Moments later, they blasted through the Bifrost and landed in the middle of New Mexico. On Earth. Climbing to their feet and dusting off their armor, the warriors looked around. In the distance, they could make out a small town. Without a word, Hogun began walking. The others shrugged. It looked as if they'd begin their search there.

"Is it just me, or does Midgard look a little different to you?" Volstagg asked.

"It has been a thousand years," Sif pointed out. "And the locals call it Earth."

Sif and the Warriors Three had not been to Earth in many, many years, and they did not know how to find Thor.

After searching the nearby town of Puente Antiguo, they got lucky. Volstagg spotted a familiar silhouette in the window of the Smith Motors building.

Inside, Thor stood next to a beautiful woman. When the woman looked up and saw Volstagg, she dropped her mug.

"Found you!" Volstagg said.

"My friends!" Thor cried, opening the door and embracing them all. Turning, he introduced them to the humans who were helping him—Jane Foster, Erik Selvig, and Darcy Lewis. Jane and Erik were scientists working on a research project in the desert, and Darcy was a college student who was assisting them.

Volstagg nodded and then introduced his companions. "Lady Sif and the Warriors Three," he said. "Surely you've heard tales of Hogun the Grim, Fandral the Dashing, and I, Volstagg the Svelte?"

Thor smiled and put a hand on his old friend's shoulder. He was glad to see them.

"We're here to take you home," Fandral said.

A light sparked in Thor's eyes and hope flooded through him.

Then, outside the window, they saw a giant hole form in the sky. The Bifrost was beginning to open again. But who—or what—was coming through this time?

Thor suspected that someone had sent Odin's most powerful weapon—the Destroyer—after him.

"Jane," he said turning to the woman beside him, "you must leave . . . now."

Jane gazed up at him. She had only known Thor a short time, but she had grown to care for this mysterious man. "What are you going to do?" she asked, scared.

"He's going to fight with us!" Volstagg cried, answering for him. Thor shook his head. He had changed during his time on Earth. He was mortal now and could not battle alongside the warriors from Asgard. But he could help Jane and the others evacuate the town.

The sky drew darker as storm clouds started to swirl high above them. Thor looked at Sif and the Warriors Three thoughtfully. "Friends," Thor began, "you must prepare for battle." Then, turning toward his new companions from Earth, he said, "It is time for action."

Without hesitation, Thor raced into the street while Jane began loading people into vans and cars to get them out of town. The townsfolk thought Jane was crazy until they saw the oncoming storm. Wanting to do their part to help, Selvig ran to empty out the diner while Darcy rushed to help those at a bus station.

Soon, the town was virtually empty. The battle was about to begin. Thor turned to Jane and her friends.

"Last chance," he said. He couldn't promise they would be safe if they didn't leave right away.

"We told you, we're staying" Jane said, determined. They were not about to leave now.

Thor smiled. His new earthbound friends were proving to be just as brave and courageous as Sif and the Warriors Three.

Thor then turned to the Asgardians and gave them a knowing look. They nodded in agreement. Sif and the Warriors Three would do whatever it took to save Thor.

Determined, Thor strode into the street, finally ready to face this fearsome enemy.

But Thor knew that this battle was just the beginning. He would not fight, but that did not mean that he wouldn't defend himself. If he did join his friends in battle— and if he did indeed survive—he knew that he would then have to return to Asgard.

Thor had changed for the better—his arrogance and impulsiveness were replaced with humility and compassion—and he wanted his father to see that.

Thor also wanted to make sure that his father was safe. There was a traitor in Asgard, and that traitor threatened the safety of Thor's family, and of the entire Realm. Someone had to bring peace and justice back to Asgard. And that someone was the mighty Thor.

But that is a tale for another day. . . .